THE DARK REALM

SKOR
THE WINGED
STALLION

With special thanks to Michael Ford

To Connor Kennedy

www.beastquest.co.uk

ORCHARD BOOKS
338 Euston Road, London NW1 3BH
Orchard Books Australia
Level 17/207 Kent St, Sydney, NSW 2000

A Paperback Original
First published in Great Britain in 2008

Beast Quest is a registered trademark of Working Partners Limited
Series created by Working Partners Limited, London

Text © Working Partners Limited 2008

Cover illustration by Steve Sims © Orchard Books 2008
Inside illustrations by Brian@KJA-artists.com © Orchard Books 2008

A CIP catalogue record for this book is available
from the British Library.

ISBN 978 1 84616 998 4

9

Printed in Great Britain by J F Print Ltd.,
Sparkford, Somerset

The paper and board used in this paperback are natural recyclable
products made from wood grown in sustainable forests. The
manufacturing processes conform to the environmental regulations
of the country of origin.

Orchard Books is a division of Hachette Children's Books,
an Hachette UK company

www.hachette.co.uk

SKOR
THE WINGED
STALLION

BY ADAM BLADE

ORCHARD BOOKS

Welcome. You stand on the edge of darkness, at the gates of an awful land. This place is Gorgonia, the Dark Realm, where the sky is red, the water black and Malvel rules. Tom and Elenna – your hero and his companion – must travel here to complete the next Beast Quest.

Gorgonia is home to six of the deadliest Beasts imaginable – minotaur, winged stallion, sea monster, Gorgon hound, mighty mammoth and scorpion man. Nothing can prepare Tom and Elenna for what they are about to face. Their past victories mean nothing. Only strong hearts and determination will save them now.

Dare you follow Tom's path once more? I advise you to turn back. Heroes can be stubborn and adventures may beckon, but if you decide to stay with Tom, you must be brave and fearless. Anything less will mean certain doom.

Watch where you step…

Kerlo the Gatekeeper

PROLOGUE

Hallam peered through the gloom. He hardly dared take another step. Shafts of light danced across the rainforest floor as the canopy of leaves swayed above. Who knew what creatures lurked behind the thick trunks, or under the giant fern leaves?

He moved slowly over the mossy ground. Noises echoed between the trees – shrill shrieks and low cackles.

This place was nothing like the woodland where he and the other Gorgonian rebels used to hide. There, the worst thing a traveller might come across was a wild boar.

But the forest wasn't safe any more. Not since Malvel had closed his net round Gorgonia. His armies scoured the land for rebels, burning the villages of innocent people. There were Beasts, too. Hallam shuddered as he remembered the deaths of his two comrades. Torgor the minotaur had torn them limb from limb.

Hallam plunged on, flashing glances in the direction of every sound. His sweat-soaked clothes clung to his body. A vine brushed against the back of his neck. He reached up to brush it away, but it wriggled beneath his touch. A snake!

"Urgh!" Hallam cried out, falling backwards.

The snake landed a pace away and drew itself into a coil, hissing. Its scales were a glistening yellow, its eyes blood-red. Hallam lay on the ground, frozen with fear. The snake fixed him with its eyes, its forked tongue flickering in and out, its head swaying, before it uncoiled and slithered away.

Hallam climbed to his feet, brushing wet leaves from his tunic. He pushed on through the trees. "You'll have to more careful!" he told himself.

Hallam was so busy watching the trees for snakes that he didn't notice where he was putting his feet. The next moment he was sliding down a massive slope. The plants on either side of him were a blur as he skidded past. And then he saw what waited at the bottom.

A pit of writing vipers!

He scrambled to slow himself, but the mud was too slippery. Vines broke off in his hand. He jammed his heels into the ground. A hair's breadth from the deadly mass of snakes, he stopped.

The blood thumped in his head, louder than the calls of the birds above.

Trembling, Hallam began to push himself back up the slope.

"You fool!" he muttered to himself. "Malvel's soldiers will find you if you don't watch your step!"

He didn't take his eyes off the snakes. He wanted to get out of the rainforest as quickly as possible.

His back came up against a tree trunk. He gripped the bark with his palms, and then felt something soft, like…feathers. Hot breath misted the air above his head.

Hallam spun round.

A horse's head pushed through the branches above him. But this was no ordinary horse. It towered over Hallam and stared down at him. A Beast! Hallam gasped for breath, his stomach turning over with fear. The creature's lips drew back, revealing a set of yellow teeth, dripping with strings of saliva.

Hallam fell to his knees at the Beast's golden hooves. Huge wings opened from the stallion's body, lifting it above the ground. The creature swayed among the trees, its powerful legs kicking, then it pulled back its head and screeched as Hallam cowered on the ground. Silver sparks flashed from the Beast's

eyes, lighting up the glossy leaves of
the jungle, before the fearsome teeth
began to close in…

CHAPTER ONE

VISION IN THE WATER

"We have to clean you up," said Elenna.

Tom and his friend stood beside the river that wound through the dusty Gorgonian plains. It was nothing like the clear streams of Avantia. Here the water was brown and sludgy. Every so often, bubbles escaped to the surface, bursting and filling the air with rotten-smelling yellow gas.

Elenna dabbed the gashes on Tom's arm where Torgor the minotaur's mighty axe had wounded him. The enchanted talon in Tom's shield, given to him by Epos the flame bird, ran out of power before it could heal all of his injuries. It had been Tom's toughest fight yet, but he had managed to free Tagus the horse-man from the clutches of Torgor. Now the good Beast was safely back in Avantia, away from Malvel's evil.

"Do you think the herbs will work?" asked Tom.

Elenna smiled as she ground up the herbs Tom's aunt had given them. Mixed with some water from her flask, they became a thick paste. Silver the wolf watched as she worked the paste into Tom's wounds.

"Thank you," he said. He didn't know how he would have survived without Elenna on his Quests.

The pain in his arm began to ebb away.

"It's working!" he cried.

The memory of the battle would take longer to fade, though. Torgor was more deadly than any Beast they had faced before. If there were other such creatures in Gorgonia, Tom knew he would need all his strength and courage to defeat them.

Elenna was bandaging the last of the linen dressings over Tom's gashes when Silver leaped to his feet and began pacing along the riverbank, barking wildly at the water.

Tom's horse Storm stamped his hooves and shook his mane, then backed away from the river's edge.

"What's got into Storm and Silver?"
asked Elenna.

"Something's spooking them," said
Tom. He peered into the water. The
current seemed to have stopped.
Silver let out a high-pitched whine
as a ripple appeared in the middle of
the water.

The two friends gazed into the river
as the patterns there shifted.
Gradually they could make out the
lines of a mouth, then a nose, then
two eyes. Ripples like long white
hairs framed the image. The mouth
moved in little waves.

Elenna gasped.

"Aduro!" said Tom.

It was their friend, the good wizard
of Avantia.

"Greetings, Tom and Elenna," the
vision in the water called.

"Greetings," they replied.

"Once again, congratulations on overcoming Torgor," said Aduro. "Tagus sends his thanks from Avantia."

Elenna squeezed Tom's arm, and Aduro continued.

"But, as you know, my magic is weak here in Gorgonia – the gateway between worlds saps my energy.

I don't have the power to stay with you long."

"Tell us, Aduro," said Tom, "what is our next mission?"

"You must track down a new Beast," said Aduro. "Its name is Skor."

Tom shot Elenna a look. She shrugged, looking mystified.

Aduro's face began to blur at the edges, and his words became distant. His magic was fading. "Beware," he whispered. "I give you a final warning: danger will come from both earth and air. Remember, earth and air..."

The face melted back into the water.

"He's gone!" cried Tom.

"What is Skor?" said Elenna. "How can it be a danger by earth and air?"

"I don't know," said Tom, "but we

have to find out. We already know that Epos is in danger." After the defeat of Torgor, the flame bird's talon in Tom's shield had begun to glow, calling for their help.

Tom picked up his shield, swung it onto his back, and tightened the magic belt around his waist. One of the belt's slots already contained the red jewel he had captured from Torgor. It gave him the ability to understand what the Beasts were thinking. But there were five slots left to fill. Tom wondered what new powers he would gain on this Quest.

"Let's see where we have to head next," Tom suggested.

Elenna opened the bag on Storm's saddle and pulled out the map given to them by Malvel. Unlike the enchanted parchment that had guided them in Avantia, this map was scrawled on animal hide. Tom shuddered as he helped Elenna unroll the greasy yellow surface.

"Look!" said Elenna. "A path."

The stench of the map was overpowering, and Tom held his breath as he leaned in closer. A green line became clear against the discoloured surface. It marked a route from their present location on the plains. The line snaked around steep rocky gullies and ravines, and ended in a place marked with tall trees many miles away. They could see the figure of a tiny flame bird hidden within the trees.

"It's a rainforest! And there's Epos," said Tom.

"It looks dangerous." Elenna sounded worried.

Tom put his hand on her shoulder. "We've overcome thirteen Beasts already," he said. "We can do it if we work together."

"We don't even know if we can trust the map," said Elenna. "Malvel may be leading us to our deaths."

Tom nodded. "Whatever Malvel throws at us, we'll be prepared," he said, rolling up the map. He gazed beyond the river. "Epos needs our help. We won't fail!"

CHAPTER TWO

TOWARDS DANGER

Storm galloped across the dusty
plains, Silver bounding tirelessly by
his side. Gorgonia's sun was hidden
behind thick banks of swirling red
cloud, and the gloom seemed to press
down upon them, ready to swallow
them up. The stallion's hooves
struggled to find a grip on the
crumbling soil, and twice he nearly

fell. But Tom gripped Storm's flanks with his legs, watching the terrain to avoid any loose rocks.

"It makes me miss Avantia," said Elenna, over the pounding of Storm's hooves. "This feels like a land of..."

"Death?" finished Tom.

Elenna shivered, as though a chill had run down her spine. There was no sign of life anywhere in Malvel's kingdom, and the stench of decay filled the air. It was as though the Dark Wizard himself was following them, breathing down their necks.

Something appeared on the horizon. Tom felt his heartbeat quicken. He tightened Storm's reins, slowing the stallion to a canter, and he felt Elenna grip his waist. But his pulse steadied as he saw it was only a dead tree.

The tree looked like a skeletal hand, reaching upwards from the earth. Its branches were leafless and decayed, and a huge vulture with patchy brown feathers perched on one of them. As they trotted past, it swivelled its bald head and fixed them with an evil stare. Tom could feel the scavenger's eyes watching them as they moved away. Silver barked nervously.

"One of Malvel's spies?" Elenna whispered into Tom's ear.

"Who knows?" Tom said, trying not to shudder.

Soon they came to a small watering hole, which looked a little cleaner than the river. Tom and Elenna dismounted and took out their flasks, while Storm trotted over to the water's edge. He bowed his head to drink, then sniffed and neighed. Silver flattened his ears and growled.

"What's the matter, boy?" asked Elenna. Then she spotted something on the far side of the pool. "Urgh!" she cried, and pointed.

A white ribcage, picked clean of flesh, broke the surface of the water. Flies buzzed over it.

"What do you think that was?" asked Elenna.

"I don't know," Tom replied, "but this water isn't safe. I'd rather be parched than poisoned."

Remounting Storm, Tom stroked his mane. "I know you're thirsty, boy, but we've got to keep going."

Storm threw back his head and shook his mane, letting out a whinny. Tom dug in his heels and the stallion shot forwards once again.

They made good speed across the plains. Ahead, the air shimmered with heat, and Tom could see nothing but pale brown earth, with an occasional spiky gorse bush. But a tingle in his stomach told him something was wrong.

After a while the gorse bushes became thicker, and Tom had to keep his eyes on the ground to steer Storm through safely. He was worried. Was

Malvel driving them into the middle of nowhere, where starvation and thirst would wear them down?

"Look out!" yelled Elenna.

Tom saw a cliff edge right in front of them. He pulled back on Storm's reins as hard as he could, and the horse let out a terrified neigh, tossing his head in panic, his hooves skidding towards the edge of the drop and throwing up clouds of dust.

"He doesn't have enough time to stop!" Tom shouted.

They were going over the edge!

CHAPTER THREE

INTO THE GORGE

Storm's body arched under the saddle as he reared back, his front hooves wheeling in the air. Pebbles clattered down into the gulley below, and the edge of the cliff started to crumble. Elenna's fingers dug into Tom's side and he felt his weight shift backwards. He lost his hold on the reins. But somehow Storm's hooves found a grip. Tom heard a thump on the ground behind him, and when he looked he could see that Elenna had fallen to safety.

But twisting round in the saddle made Tom lose his balance. He tried to grab Storm's mane to steady himself, but it was too late. He was falling! The empty valley opened up below him, as rocks and pebbles scattered. His body knocked into the side of the cliff...then pain jolted through his ankle. He was suspended in the air, his arms dangling. His cheeks were grazed by the rough stones, but he was alive.

"Storm's stirrup!" Tom shouted. "It saved me!"

But he hardly dared to move. Only his foot, caught in the stirrup, stopped him from hurtling into the depths of the canyon. Even the magic token in his shield that protected him from falls might not be able to help him in a ravine as deep as this.

Elenna poked her head over the cliff edge. "Hold on!" she shouted.

"I'm not going anywhere," said Tom.

Then he heard her talking to Storm. "That's right, boy, slowly," she coaxed, encouraging the stallion to walk away from the cliff edge and pull Tom back up to solid ground. But he knew they would have to go slowly – Elenna didn't want his foot to slip loose from the stirrup.

Gradually, Tom felt himself being heaved up the cliff. As soon as he approached solid ground, he twisted round and used his arms to scramble to safety. Then he pulled his foot from the stirrup and lay back on the dusty earth, gasping with relief. Silver licked his face excitedly, and he reached out a hand to pat the wolf's neck.

"Thank you, Elenna!" he panted. Storm whinnied. "And you too," Tom added.

The stallion's flanks were slick with sweat and his legs trembled. Elenna whispered gently in his ear, reassuring him. "There, there, boy, it's all right."

She stepped over to gaze down into the ravine. "Do you think anything lives down there?" she asked, her voice echoing among the rocks below.

"I don't know, but we must get across to rescue Epos," said Tom. He pointed to the trees on the other side of the gorge. "That has to be the rainforest."

"Can you jump across, using the power of your golden boots?" Elenna asked.

Tom shook his head. "Here the gorge is as wide as ten houses," he said grimly. "The magic wouldn't be strong enough."

Tom scanned the distance with his keen sight, one of the powers he had won during his Quest to find the golden armour. He spotted something dark looping across the gorge. A bridge! It looked narrow and flimsy, but it was the only choice they had.

"I can see a bridge," he said. "We can cross there."

He swung himself back into Storm's saddle and offered a hand to Elenna. She was pale.

"What's the matter?" Tom asked.

His friend frowned, peering down into the gulley. "We're going to have to be careful," she said. "Those rocks could be deadly."

Tom climbed down from Storm and placed both hands on her shoulders. "We've battled thirteen beasts and won," he said. "I know you have the strength to meet this challenge."

Elenna looked up, and Tom saw her face had changed. Her eyes shone with fierce determination.

"Let's do it," she said.

The two of them scrambled into Storm's saddle, and Tom steered his horse in a gallop towards the bridge. Silver's fur flattened as he bounded beside them.

When the bridge drew near, Tom slowed Storm to a canter.

"I've seen stronger bridges!" Elenna joked, trying to smile.

Tom felt doubt tighten in his throat. The bridge that spanned the gorge looked ancient. The rope rails were thin and frayed, and the wooden planks were black with age. Then he remembered the gift given to him by the golden chainmail – strength of heart.

"It's the only way for both of us to cross," he said. "But Storm is too heavy – the bridge won't hold him. He'll have to stay here with Silver."

"Yes," Elenna agreed. Tom felt her twist in the saddle. "Where is Silver?"

Tom spun round. The wolf was nowhere to be seen.

"Silver!" shouted Elenna. "Where are you?"

A howl sounded from behind a nearby cluster of boulders. They leaped off Storm, dashed in the direction of the noise and found Silver. He was sniffing a bush loaded with bright red berries.

"Food!" said Elenna. "Clever boy, Silver." She ruffled his fur, then started to pick the fruit.

Tom joined her. It had been so long since they last ate. Tom stuffed the juicy berries into his mouth until the sticky sweet juice dribbled down his chin.

"They taste so good," Elenna laughed, licking her fingers. "Who would have thought something so delicious could grow in Gorgonia?"

Tom stopped. Elenna was right. The berries tasted *too* good. He spat out his mouthful, and stared at his friend. Elenna was blurring in front of him. Tom held up his hand in front of his face – his fingers became hazy round the edges. He staggered sideways.

"The berries!" he said. "They're poisonous!"

It was another of Malvel's evil tricks, sent to stop their Quest.

Elenna stumbled towards him. "What shall we do?" she asked.

Tom pointed shakily to the gorge. "We have to get across the bridge – while we still can."

Holding onto each other, they hurried unsteadily towards the edge of the cliff. Storm came to their side.

"You'll have to stay here," said

Tom, unhooking his shield from the stallion's saddle and patting the horse's head.

Silver lifted his nose and licked Elenna's hand.

"You too, Silver," she murmured.

The wolf dropped back, letting out a worried whine.

Tom edged towards the bridge. It was narrow and he felt so unsteady on his feet.

"We'll have to go one at a time," he said. "Let me lead the way."

A strong wind had picked up, gusting along the gorge. The rope bridge swayed and creaked. Tom shuddered. None of his special powers could help him now. He looked back to Storm and Silver. Both animals were watching in silence.

"Maybe we should wait until the

poison wears off," suggested Elenna, tightening her grip on Tom's arm.

"We don't have time," he replied. "Somewhere in that rainforest, Epos needs our help."

"You're right," said Elenna.

Pulling away from his friend's arm, Tom stepped onto the bridge.

CHAPTER FOUR

CROSSING THE BRIDGE

"Be careful!" said Elenna. "Don't go too fast."

The bridge groaned under Tom's weight. His vision blurred again, and he shot out a hand to steady himself against the ropes. He managed to take another short step.

Then a screech made him glance up. A black shape drifted under the clouds. Tom's eyes regained focus. An eagle! It circled, suspended on the air, gliding gracefully through the red sky. It screeched again, the noise piercing Tom's brain.

Was this another of Malvel's tricks? A distraction to send him plummeting to his death?

Tom gripped the ropes and inched his way across the bridge. Each time he took another step, the ropes creaked, but somehow the bridge held. Tom's dizziness was becoming worse, though. The wind was stronger now, whipping through his hair.

Shaking his head to clear his thoughts, Tom called back to Elenna. "It's safe," he shouted. The wind snatched his breath away. Had she heard him? He yelled again. "The ropes are strong enough! You can come across."

He looked round to see Elenna place a foot on the bridge. So far, so good. But as Elenna took another step, Tom realised he had made a mistake. The bridge began to swing to one side, then the other. The weight of both of them, plus the strong wind, was making the bridge sway dangerously.

Tom bent down, keeping his weight close to the wooden planks. The bridge lurched alarmingly. Was Elenna all right?

He turned round to check. Elenna was making good progress towards him, but the bridge was still swinging violently. Tom began to back towards the end, keeping his eyes on Elenna.

"You're doing well," he called

encouragingly. "You're nearly in the middle."

Elenna flashed a weak smile. Then she tripped. She thrust a hand out to break her fall, only just keeping hold of the rope with her other hand. A shudder travelled along the bridge like a wave, tilting it to one side. Tom was thrown against the ropes and cried out in terror. He barely managed to hold on.

"Are you all right?" shouted Elenna.

"I think so!" shouted Tom. "Keep coming towards me."

He felt something slimy against his palm and looked more closely at the rope he was holding. What he saw made him feel sick. It was made of hair! Many different colours, all wound tightly together. Was it hair from long-dead Beasts? Or human

hair? Who knew what evil Malvel
was capable of!

The eagle screeched again, closer

this time. Tom watched its black shape swoop low over the bridge. Was it watching them?

Elenna had reached Tom now, and the wind had died down. They were going to make it.

"Nearly there," he said, taking her arm. Then Tom noticed the rope on his left give a tiny shudder. He looked back. The eagle was perched on the far end of the bridge. Gripping the rope between its talons, it tore at the strands with its beak.

"No!" shouted Tom.

Elenna turned round in horror.

Tom didn't have time to answer. Before the eagle was halfway through the twine, there was a loud twang and the rope snapped.

Tom felt his feet fall away and his

whole world turned upside down.
He and Elenna plunged into the air,
their screams echoing through the
rocky gorge.

CHAPTER FIVE

ESCAPE FROM THE GORGE

The rock face rushed past. But soon Tom felt himself begin to slow. *Of course! My shield!* he thought. Its magic was protecting him – but would it slow him enough to avoid crashing into the rocks below?

As he passed a ledge, Tom shot out a hand. Jagged rock cut into his fingers, but he held on. His whole body jarred. Elenna was falling towards him, spiralling through the air. He would only get one chance…

He reached out, his fingers closing around her wrist.

"Got you!" he said. The extra weight tore at his muscles, but he couldn't let his friend fall.

Elenna's nails dug into his wrist as she clung to him. Gathering all his strength, Tom heaved her up so she could reach the ledge, then pulled himself up onto it. Thankfully, the evil poison that had blurred his vision seemed to be wearing off and he was able to see what he was doing.

He lay on the ground, panting for breath.

"Thanks," gasped Elenna. "You saved my life."

"How is your eyesight?" asked Tom.

Elenna moved her hand in front of her face, flexing her fingers. "It's better! Malvel's magic is wearing off."

Tom gazed up. The top of the gorge was far above them.

"How will we get out?" asked Elenna.

"We'll have to climb," said Tom.

But the sides of the gulley were slick with slime. With no ropes, it would be difficult.

Tom hauled himself up against the rock face and placed his foot against a shallow dent. Keeping his body tight against the rock, he began to pick a path upwards, using the tiny crevices to lever his way.

"One step at a time," he called down to Elenna. "Slowly and carefully."

Elenna pulled herself up behind him.

Tom's knuckles turned white, and sweat streamed down his back. He forced himself to concentrate. Reach. Step. Reach. Step. Up there, somewhere, Epos the flame bird needed help.

The muscles in his arms and chest

ached and his legs shook, but Tom pushed onwards. Then he saw it – a rope. It was the frayed remains of the hair-cord from the bridge, dangling into the abyss. Tom tugged hard on the end. It held.

"We can use this," he called down to Elenna.

He seized the rope and began to haul himself up, his feet pushing against the slope. Placing hand over hand, he dragged himself up the final section of the cliff. Behind him, he could hear Elenna breathing hard. When he got to the top, Tom leaned back to help his friend. Then they collapsed together in the dirt.

"We've made it!" Elenna gasped.

Tom turned to face the rainforest. Huge trees shot out of the earth. Their luscious green leaves cast the undergrowth into shadow. He could make out vines wrapped around the tree trunks and snaking tendrils hanging from the branches.

"Come on!" said Tom. "Let's make Aduro proud of us."

They hurried towards the forest. Smaller trees grew at the edges, with twisted, leafless branches that seemed to reach out as they passed by. Bushes, sprouting stems lined with thorns, tore at their legs. Parts of the ground were marshy, and Tom felt squelching mud clutch at his feet. Then he noticed something strange. A patch of long swamp-grass was crushed. He walked another few steps and saw another flattened area.

"Look, Elenna," he cried. "They're shaped like…"

"Hooves," Elenna finished.

Tom nodded slowly. "But they must be ten times the size of Storm's hoofprints! What creature could have feet that large?"

Elenna didn't answer and Tom shot her a glance. She wasn't even looking at him. Her eyes, opened wide, were fixed on a spot behind his head. Her hand shook as she pointed.

"Skor!" she yelled.

CHAPTER SIX

AN ENEMY RETURNS

Tom froze. A horse's body, as black as coal, towered above him. Silver sparks flashed from its eyes. The Beast reared on muscular hind legs, churning the air with gleaming golden hooves. His mane was as white as snow and his tail floated in the air like strands of emerald seaweed.

Skor gave a deafening roar and unfurled giant, glossy wings. He launched himself into the air. Tom staggered backwards into Elenna. The underside of the Beast's feathers shimmered purple like an exotic seashell and the tips looked as if they had been dipped in gold. Tom spotted a shimmer of emerald green in one of the golden hooves. A jewel the size of his fist was embedded there, just like the red gem in Torgor's axe.

Skor beat his mighty wings back and forth, diving low over Tom and Elenna, his huge wings slicing the air above their heads. Then the wheeling hooves crashed back to the ground, sending tremors through the earth that knocked Tom to his knees.

Skor snorted, but didn't come

forwards. Then a voice pierced
the stillness.

"Very good," it said. "It is right that
you should bow before me."

Tom saw a figure jump down from
Skor's back. He recognised him right
away. The boy was a year or two
older than Tom, with pale blond hair.
A bronze sword hung by his side.

"Seth!"

"That's right," said the boy. "Didn't
you expect to see me again?"

Tom had met Seth once before, on a Quest to save Vedra and Krimon, two baby dragons. But that had been another time, in another kingdom.

"How did you get to—" he began.

"Gorgonia?" Seth finished the question for him. "I'll always be able to find you."

Tom climbed to his feet and drew his sword. *I'll finish the fight this time*, he told himself.

Seth's lip curled into a sneer when he saw Tom's blade. He unsheathed his own. "I hoped I would get the chance to fight you again," he said. Then he turned to Skor and pointed back into the forest with his sword.

"Be gone, Skor! Do Malvel's bidding, and take care of our prisoner."

The Beast snorted and rose into the

air. Then it headed back into the depths of the forest, its wing-tips glittering like flames.

Tom tightened his hand around his shield's strap. He pushed Elenna back among the foliage, whispering, "Stay out of the way." Then he raised his voice.

"What have you done to Avantia's Beast?"

Seth laughed. "You won't see her again."

Tom clenched his teeth. "You're nothing but Malvel's puppet."

"That's better than being Aduro's work-horse," Seth shot back.

Tom adjusted his grip, raised his sword and darted forwards, cutting through the air.

Seth stepped aside nimbly, grinning. "This will be easier than

I thought," he said.

He lunged at Tom, who parried
with a downward stroke. Seth struck
again, slicing an arc at Tom's legs.
Tom jumped, feeling the draught of
the blade pass under his feet. Seth's
face was red and he hissed in anger,
then brought his blade down heavily.

Tom blocked upwards with his shield, feeling the power of the blow shoot through his arm. Seth grunted. Tom tried to thrust underneath him, but Seth parried, and their blades jammed together. They glared at each other, locked in position, faces close enough for Tom to feel the warmth of Seth's breath.

"You can't keep this up for ever," said Seth through gritted teeth.

"I won't stop until it's over," vowed Tom, then he thrust his shield into Seth's stomach. They both toppled to the ground, but Tom was up first. "Let your sword do the talking," he said, watching as Seth climbed to his feet, his face black with anger.

His enemy ran forwards, shouting furiously, and swinging wildly with his sword. It whistled through the air, but Tom kept his shield well placed. He backed away until he saw his chance. He ducked under one of Seth's swings and twisted up behind him. With his right hand he pinned Seth's sword arm. With his left he held his blade to his enemy's throat.

"You've lost!" he said in Seth's ear. "Drop your sword."

Seth's blade clattered to the ground. Tom kicked it to Elenna. But as her fingers closed over the hilt, a high-pitched screech rang out through the air. It filled Tom's head and he had to let go of Seth to cover his ears. He could barely stay on his feet.

Just as abruptly, the screeching ceased. Seth was already running in the direction of the rainforest, but Tom didn't care about him any more. He knew that the awful sound was a Beast in pain. The flame bird's talon, fixed into his shield, was vibrating and glowing, and through the red jewel in his belt, which helped him to understand the thoughts of Avantia's Beasts, he realised that time was running out for Epos.

CHAPTER SEVEN

FINDING THE FLAME BIRD

They dashed towards the rainforest.
Seth had disappeared into the
shadows ahead of them. But Tom
couldn't give chase; he had to get
to Epos.

The trees were massive, the trunks
taller than the towers of King Hugo's
castle and some as wide as five men.

A figure appeared suddenly from

behind one of the trees. Tom recognised his bald head and eye-patch. It was the keeper of the gate between Avantia and Gorgonia.

"Look, Elenna!" he said. "It's Kerlo."

They watched the ragged figure hobble towards them, supported by his wooden staff. Kerlo paused when he was still some distance away. He smiled and lifted his hand.

"Greetings, travellers!" he called out. "How fares your journey?"

"We have to rescue Epos," shouted Tom. "She's trapped in the forest."

Kerlo nodded slowly. "I warned you, did I not? Gorgonia doesn't welcome fools."

Tom felt his fists clench. "We're not fools, gatekeeper. We have a Quest to fulfil."

"The jungle holds many dangers,

young one. You will need great bravery," said Kerlo. He shook his head.

Tom was tired of the gatekeeper's mocking tone. "We're not afraid of anything," he said.

"That's funny," Kerlo replied. "Your father Taladon said the same thing to me once."

Taladon! Tom had never met his father, who had disappeared before Tom was born, but the stories of his brave deeds seemed to have reached the furthest corners of Avantia – and Gorgonia. Kerlo turned to leave.

"Wait!" said Tom. "Tell me more!"

Epos screeched again, but more faintly this time.

"Come on, Tom," said Elenna. "We don't have much time. She's losing strength."

He nodded. And when he looked back, Kerlo was gone.

They turned and plunged into the foliage. The air in the forest was thick and heavy. It was dark, too, and the shadows shifted as though creatures were creeping through the gloom. Suddenly Elenna seized Tom's arm.

"What's that?" she whispered, pointing.

Tom couldn't see anything but dense leaves.

"What?" he asked.

Elenna relaxed. "I thought I saw something…a pair of eyes."

Tom peered again, and felt a chill tingling down his spine.

"Just stay close," he said.

The ground was covered in spongy moss, and huge fallen branches blocked the path ahead. Mysterious sounds came from all around them – the shrill calls of unseen animals cutting through the air. The leaves above them rustled, but when Tom looked, he could see nothing. Somewhere in the distance a branch splintered. Tom couldn't shake the feeling that they were being watched. But Seth was nowhere to be seen.

"I wish Silver was with us," said Elenna.

Tom thought about Storm, too, and

tried to ignore how heavy his heart felt without their loyal friends.

As they moved further into the jungle, the vines became thicker. Tom drew his sword and hacked them aside. The canopy above them blocked out most of the red sunlight. A black shape suddenly broke cover, and shot between their heads. Elenna grabbed her bow and Tom spun round with his sword.

"It's only a bat," said Elenna, relieved. "It won't hurt us."

Epos's cries were fading now, but the talon in Tom's shield vibrated more strongly than ever. If they didn't find the Beast soon, perhaps they never would. Tom couldn't let that happen. *I won't let Aduro down*, he promised himself.

Then his eyes fell on a low branch.

It was splintered in the centre, the end hanging loose. He walked nearer. The ground was trampled with a huge hoof-print.

"Skor must have come this way," he whispered. "Let's follow his tracks – they should lead us to Epos."

They edged forwards, keeping close together. Skor's tracks cut through the forest. Small trees had been torn from the earth and plants crushed.

Soon they reached a clearing. Tom peered between the trees.

"Careful," he said, holding up a hand in front of Elenna. "It might be a trap."

But there she was! Epos the flame bird. The good Beast sat in a makeshift nest of giant leaves. But her feathers weren't the same burnished gold that Tom remembered. They were a dirty

brown. And her eyes no longer
burned like molten iron. As she
shifted in her nest, Tom could see that
one wing wasn't folding properly. It
stuck out from her body at an
awkward angle. From the twisted and
missing feathers, Tom realised that the
bones must be broken.

"She can't fly," said Tom. "She's
completely helpless."

Tears welled in Elenna's eyes. "She
must be in terrible pain!"

"It's Malvel's work," Tom said,
feeling his anger rise. "And his evil
helper Seth."

They broke cover and walked
towards the stricken Beast. When
Epos spotted them approaching, she
lifted her beak and gave a soft caw.

"There, there," soothed Tom.

"Do you think the magical talon

will be powerful enough to heal her injuries?" asked Elenna.

"I don't know," said Tom. "It's never had to heal anything this bad."

They had almost reached the nest when a rustling came from the far side of the clearing. Tom and Elenna froze.

The leaves began to shake wildly, and tremors stirred the ground beneath their feet.

Golden hooves crashed through the foliage and giant wings beat the air.

It was Skor!

CHAPTER EIGHT

FACING THE WINGED STALLION

The Beast burst through the trees, cracking small trees like twigs. Epos lifted her head and let out a terrified squawk.

Seth ran out from behind Skor, his sword held in front of him. Tom didn't have time to draw his weapon.

Luckily, Elenna was quicker. She shoved a foot in Seth's path, and sent him stumbling to the ground. He was climbing back to his feet when she swung a branch at him. It crunched into Seth's temple, and he crumpled to the forest floor beside Epos's nest.

Tom cut down a vine and threw it to Elenna. "Tie him up with this!" he called.

Elenna was on Seth in a flash, and bound his wrists with the vine.

"Quickly, Tom," she shouted. "There isn't much time. The vines won't hold him for long."

A roar filled the clearing and Tom turned to face Skor. The Beast drew back his lips. Huge yellow teeth snapped the air and the Beast flew up over the trees.

Tom dashed away from the flame bird's nest. He wanted to put as much distance as possible

between Skor and Epos.

He was halfway across the clearing when the winged stallion dived at him. Tom ducked and was surrounded by the Beast's stinking breath.

"Over here!" shouted Seth furiously.

Tom spun round to see that Skor's attention had turned to Elenna, who was pinning Seth to the ground. The Beast flew towards her, eyes flashing silver sparks onto the forest floor.

"Hey!" Tom shouted. "Leave her alone!"

Epos bravely tried to lift herself out of her nest, but sank back defeated. Tom picked up a rock from the ground, and took careful aim. Skor was almost on top of Elenna now, and she scrambled back from Seth, who writhed on the ground. Tom threw the rock and it hit the side of Skor's head.

The Beast crashed to the ground, snorting in pain and anger. He charged towards Tom once more. There was no time to think, and nowhere to run. All Tom could do was roll out of the way. He found himself hidden behind a thick tree trunk.

Elenna, meanwhile, had returned to Seth's side.

"Leave him, Elenna!" Tom shouted. "You have to hide."

She looked up, and then back at Seth, uncertainty written on her face. Then she seized their enemy under the armpits and began dragging him towards the edge of the clearing, away from Epos's nest.

Tom heard the crunch of Skor's hooves in the undergrowth, and flattened himself against the trunk. There was no way he could face this Beast on the forest floor. He wouldn't even be able to get close to Skor's head. Maybe if he could get higher...

Tom looked up the trunk.

Skor appeared at the side of the tree, sniffing the air. The purple feathers of his wings ruffled, and his flanks rose and fell.

Tom edged around the trunk, keeping out of the Beast's sight, then began to climb. The bark of the tree was coarse and cracked, with plenty of handholds, and Tom was as high as Skor's back when the Beast finally spotted him.

Skor's eyes opened wide and sparks flashed against the trunk, burning the wood. Then the Beast opened his mouth and roared. The yellow teeth snapped at Tom, but he managed to pull his legs out of the way. He drew his sword and swung it at the winged stallion. It glanced off Skor's head, but did no damage at all.

"Climb higher!" shouted Elenna from below. "You have to get above him."

Tom scrambled up to a hollow in the trunk, and climbed into it. Skor tried to unfurl his wings, but the trees were too dense. The Beast retreated to the bottom of the tree, out of sight. For a moment, Tom felt safe.

Then the branches began to tremble, as though a strong wind were blowing through them.

"Get out, Tom!" Elenna screamed from below. Tom caught sight of her terrified face through the leaves. She was sheltering by another tree, her foot resting on Seth's back.

Then Tom realised what was happening. The Beast was tearing down the tree!

"You have to climb down!" shouted Elenna.

The Beast attacked the trunk again, and the branches where Tom was crouched shook wildly, scattering leaves below. The whole tree creaked.

Tom sheathed his sword and started to scramble down. But it was too late. The tree leaned over, swinging wildly one way, then the other. Tom felt his stomach lurch.

A loud splintering sound echoed in the clearing and the trunk began to topple, scything through the foliage. Green leaves blurred past Tom's eyes. He had only one chance. He pushed off with his feet and jumped. The ground rushed towards him.

Tom landed on the mossy carpet, bending his knees to cushion the blow, and rolled away. Behind him, the tree slammed into the forest floor. Birds shrieked and dirt filled his eyes.

Skor was already galloping towards him through the debris. Tom drew his sword. He lifted his shield and threw himself at the golden hooves. They thudded against the wood of his shield as he swung his sword, slashing Skor's leg.

The Beast took a few steps backwards – and to Tom's horror, the wound disappeared before his eyes. The skin was unblemished again.

"A Beast that doesn't bleed?" shouted Tom in confusion. "How am I supposed to defeat it?"

"You didn't think Malvel would make it easy, did you?" Seth cackled. "Face it, you and Epos are going to die!"

"Aim for the head!" shouted Elenna. "It's the only way to stop him."

As the Beast kicked out, Tom dodged sideways to avoid the blow. If reaching Skor's head was the only way to save Epos, that was what he would have to do. *But how can I get close enough?* he thought desperately.

As Skor reared again, Tom saw his chance. He darted under the wheeling hooves and threw himself at Skor's rear leg, wrapping his arms around it. Skor snorted and bucked, kicking out with both his back legs. Tom felt his teeth rattle in his head, and his sword fell from his grasp.

"Tom!" cried Elenna.

His hands came loose and he was thrown through the air. He smashed into the ground among the leaves of the fallen tree, and a sharp pain stung his forehead. Blood trickled into his eye.

Skor thrashed at the ground with his hooves, then charged towards him, spreading his dazzling wings and lifting from the ground. As he hovered in the air, strings of saliva drooled from his jaws.

"Kill Tom!" bellowed Seth.

"Tom, get up!" shouted Elenna.

Tom struggled to his feet, and faced Skor. The Beast's wingtips scattered golden rays of light across the clearing. Tom looked around for his sword, or something else to fight back with. There was nothing. But Tom wouldn't give up. Not now – not after all they had been through.

As the Beast's hooves sliced towards his face, Tom pushed out his shield. "While there's blood in my veins," he yelled, "Malvel will never triumph!"

CHAPTER NINE

FIGHT TO THE END

Skor's hooves crunched onto Tom's shield, but he kept his arm firm and the wood held. Then Skor whinnied in pain. Tom peered round from behind his shield, and saw an arrow sticking out of Skor's flank.

"Elenna!" he cried.

His friend had left Seth's side and was hurrying towards them, stringing another arrow.

"Run, Tom!" she shouted. "I can't hold him back for long."

Tom looked around. There must be something he could do.

Elenna unleashed a second arrow, which embedded itself under Skor's mane. The Beast backed off again,

but already the first arrow had dropped out, and the skin had healed.

Tom's eyes fell on a reed-filled swamp at the edge of the clearing, and an idea formed in his head. He thought about the way that Elenna had whispered in Storm's ear. Then he remembered a story his uncle had once told him about horse whisperers – people who could calm whole herds of stampeding animals by blowing through pampas grasses. Perhaps the same thing would work with these reeds.

Tom scrambled towards the swamp.

"Stop him!" shouted Seth.

Tom looked back and saw that Elenna was pulling another arrow from her quiver. She only had three left.

The swamp was green and the

water was as thick as tar. Tom strode into the centre of the reeking pond. The warm sludge swallowed his legs up to the knee. He tugged at the nearest reed, wincing as the sharp edge cut into his hand. He pulled again, and the reed came free.

"I've got no arrows left!" shouted Elenna.

Skor was thundering towards her.

Tom placed the reed between his hands and blew into his palms.

A note like a shrill scream rang out across the rainforest clearing. Elenna dropped her bow and crouched on the floor, clutching her hands to her ears. Epos gave a cry and sank her head into the side of the nest.

Skor stopped a few paces from Elenna, and lowered his hooves. His eyes sparkled, but no longer sent their lightning bolts into the foliage.

It's working, thought Tom. He took a lungful of air and blew again.

Skor shook his white mane as though getting rid of a nuisance fly. Then his eyelids drooped and his green tail hung limply.

"No!" shouted Seth. "Curse you both!"

Tom gave a final blow on the reed, and Skor's head sank to his chest. He stood completely still.

"Tom," whispered Elenna, pointing. "Your sword!"

There it was, resting at the base of a tree. Tom dropped the reed and ran to it. Holding the weapon in his hand, he approached Skor. The mighty Beast towered above him. Could Skor really be asleep? The feathers on his wings didn't so much as stir.

"Be careful!" whispered Elenna.

"I'll have to climb onto his back," said Tom. "I can't reach his head from here."

"No!" shouted Seth. "Wake up, Skor!"

The Beast's eyes shot open, but Tom was quick. He hurled his sword through the air with all his strength. It spiralled towards Skor, the hilt smashing into his head. The winged stallion reared on his hind legs, his mighty wings unfurling and filling the sky with their purple gleam as he shrieked with pain.

Skor's hooves did not fall back down to the ground. He remained frozen, legs raised and mouth gaping, like a statue.

"What's happening?" gasped Elenna.

A green glow began to creep up Skor's back legs. It was as though the forest was reaching out and claiming the Beast. Tom had seen this already with Torgor the minotaur. As green crystals began to form over the winged stallion's body, Tom leaped out of the way.

A giant emerald prison closed over the Beast. Elenna gave a low whistle of awe. Then Epos sounded a warning squawk.

"Quick!" shouted Elenna. "Seth's escaping."

Tom saw Seth running away, his hands still tied behind his back. Another vine, broken in the centre, trailed from his ankles. Elenna chased after him, and had almost caught their enemy when she tripped and fell into the dirt. Seth took his chance. He dived into the shadows between the trees and was gone.

"He must have cut himself free while I was helping you," said Elenna. "I'm sorry…"

"It's not your fault," said Tom, placing a hand on Elenna's shoulder. He stared into the forest. "Though I'm sure that's not the last we've seen of Seth."

Together they walked back to Skor.

"What's that?" said Elenna, bending

down to pick up something among the long grasses. It was the green jewel from the winged stallion's hoof. "Another token for your belt, Tom."

The gemstone slipped easily into one of the five remaining notches of his belt.

"I wonder what it does?" said Tom.

A pitiful wailing interrupted them.

"Epos!" said Elenna.

The flame bird was resting her head on the side of the nest. Short, rasping breaths made her feathers shudder. She stared at Tom pleadingly through half-closed, glassy eyes.

"Quick," said Tom urgently. "We have to help her. She's dying!"

CHAPTER TEN

A RACE AGAINST TIME

Close up, Epos's wound was sickening. Forest insects were hovering over the bleeding and broken wing.

Elenna stroked the good Beast's head. "Can you help her?"

"I can try," said Tom, taking the enchanted talon from his shield. He ran it over Epos's injuries but nothing happened. He tried again.

"Curse Malvel!" said Tom. "It's not working. Perhaps it's just not strong enough."

"Tom!" cried Elenna. "Your belt!"

Tom looked down. Skor's jewel was glowing dimly.

Elenna raised her eyebrows. "Do you think…?"

Tom pulled the crystal from his belt. "There's only one way to find out!"

He held the jewel close to Epos's wounded wing. It shone more brightly the closer it came, until Tom had to shield his eyes. Soon the clearing was completely bathed in green light. Tom watched in amazement as Epos's wing moved a little. Slowly, the bones straightened out as though they were being reset by an invisible hand. Finally, feathers grew back over the bald patch where they had been torn out of the skin.

"The crystal has the power to heal broken bones!" said Tom. "Even those of a Beast!"

Epos lifted her head from the nest. The life flooded back to her eyes as she opened her beak and gave a squawk of gratitude. She spread her mighty wings and a smokeless fire broke out over the feathers. Epos the flame bird was alive and well.

"She's more incredible than ever," murmured Elenna.

With a flap of her wings, Epos sprang out of the nest and flew towards the treetops.

Tom looked up at the canopy of branches. "She won't be able to escape the forest," he said. "The trees are too dense."

But something strange happened.
As Epos rose up, a slit opened in the
air in front of her. It spread until it
was as big as Epos herself.

"A gateway!" said Elenna, turning
to Tom with wide eyes.

Tom could see blue sky. There were
huge towers of stone, too, and flags
fluttering in the breeze. He heard the
call of distant trumpets. The smell of
fresh air filled his nostrils – the smell
of home.

"It's King Hugo's castle!" he said, his heart lurching. It seemed so long since he had been home. Epos was hovering by the gateway, ready to leave. At least she could escape the terrible kingdom of Gorgonia.

Tom and Elenna waved.

"Goodbye, Epos!" Tom called. "It's time for you to see Avantia again."

The red jewel in Tom's belt glimmered, allowing him to sense the flame bird's thoughts, and he felt the warmth of Epos's farewell. He knew she was saying thank you. She squawked one final time, and flew through the hole in the sky. It closed up behind her, leaving a scattering of fiery ashes that drifted down into the clearing.

"We've done it, Tom!" said Elenna. "Another good Beast is free."

Tom nodded in the direction of Skor. "And another of Malvel's evil Beasts is defeated," he said.

"Where do you think Seth has gone?" asked Elenna.

"I don't know," said Tom. "But we need to get back to Silver and Storm. They'll be worried."

Tom and Elenna retraced their steps. The rainforest didn't seem nearly as frightening now that Skor had been defeated.

When they reached the edge of the forest they could see Silver and Storm waiting on the far side of the gorge.

"How are we going to get across?" asked Elenna in dismay. "The bridge is gone!"

The air shimmered and Aduro appeared before them. "Well done,

my friends. Allow me to help."

Tom felt himself rising into the air.
Beside him, Elenna laughed with
delight as they found themselves
swooping high over the gulley.

"I feel like a bird!" shouted Elenna.

The ground on the other side was
approaching fast.

"Brace yourself!" Tom yelled. He hit
the land hard, and sprawled in the
dirt. His shield skittered away, and

came to a rest against a nearby bush. He climbed to his feet, and looked back over the gorge – but Aduro had gone.

Elenna was laughing. "I don't think I'll ever be afraid of heights again!" she said.

Storm galloped over and nudged at Tom with his nose. Silver licked Elenna's face excitedly. Tom brushed the earth off his knees and climbed to his feet. It was good to be back together again.

He walked over to retrieve his shield. But as he turned it over, he saw that the sea serpent's tooth on its surface was glowing and vibrating. Tom turned to his companion.

"Elenna, we have to go!" he said.

"Why?" she said, worry creasing her brow.

Tom held out the shield for her to see. "It's Sepron the sea serpent."

Another of Avantia's good Beasts was in danger.

"While there's blood in my veins," Tom swore, thrusting his sword to the sky, "I'll finish this Quest!"

Join Tom on the next stage
of the Beast Quest

Meet

Narga
THE SEA MONSTER

Can Tom free the good Beasts from
the Dark Realm?

PROLOGUE

Odora stood at the stern of the ship and peered out across the Black Ocean of Gorgonia. The only light came from the purple moon, half-hidden by cloud. She and her brother Dako were trying to stay close to the coast, but the dark night and the thickening mist hid any land. There was no sign of Malvel's guards, but Odora knew that the evil wizard's men could be prowling the sea and shore.

She glanced down at the huge chest of weapons near her feet. A surge of grim satisfaction shot through her as she thought about how these arms would help the Gorgonian rebels in their fight against Malvel. But the stakes were high. If the evil wizard caught them with the smuggled weapons, he would show no mercy.

Suddenly the ship lurched. Odora staggered forwards and saved herself from falling by grabbing the ship's rail. Her heart pounding, she hurried towards the bow of the ship, where she spotted the crouching figure of Dako.

"What's happening?" she whispered.

"I haven't *seen* anything," Dako replied in a low voice. "But we're not alone. There's something out there."

Odora clenched her hands to stop them shaking with fear. "We can't get caught. If Malvel's guards find the weapons we're carrying, they'll kill us!"

Dako shot her a warning look. "Keep your voice down. We've *got* to get through with these weapons. They're our only chance against Malvel." He peered cautiously over the rail.

"Can you see anything?" Odora asked, crouching low.

Before Dako could reply, a wave flooded over the deck soaking them both. Then, out of the wave, rose a long, slender neck and a hideous, snake-like head. Terrified, the brother and sister stood rooted to the spot.

The Beast swooped down towards them, jaws agape. Odora leaped out of the way, catching a glimpse of rotting fangs and a flickering, forked tongue.

The vicious jaws grabbed Dako by the head

and lifted him clear of the ship. Her brother kicked out and pounded his fists against the Beast's scaly neck, but he couldn't free himself.

"Dako! Dako!" Odora screamed. She sprang up, reaching for her brother's legs, but he was already beyond her grasp. She saw his body go limp as the Beast vanished into the fog.

Behind her, Odora heard a second wave swirl over the deck and she spun round to see another head on a long neck rearing up out of the water. *Two Beasts!* she thought despairingly.

The second Beast stretched out towards her, jaws snapping. Odora dived away, sliding along the soaking deck until she reached the weapon chest. Throwing it open, she pulled out a sword and swung at the sea monster with all her might. The Beast's head reared away from her gleaming blade.

But five more heads were appearing out of the mist, joining the first Beast. They surrounded the ship, looming over it and snapping at Odora, their fangs long and sharp. She struck out with her sword again, but the six heads were too fast for her. They weaved to and fro, darting between her sword strokes.

Odora felt her arms grow weaker and the sword heavier.

Trying to dodge one of the heads, Odora slipped on the wet deck. As she struggled to recover her balance, the ship was raised out of the water. The deck tilted. Swords, spears and crossbows skidded across the wet planks and fell into the sea.

The heads reared up as one, and Odora gasped with terror as she saw that all the necks extended out of one huge, bulbous body. There weren't six separate Beasts, but one enormous Beast with six heads. "No!" she screamed as the creature wrapped its necks around the ship and hurled it aside as easily as if it were a pebble.

Odora was flung through the air. *I'm going to die*, she thought in the last seconds before she plunged into the black waves. *And we've failed. Without the weapons the rebels have no chance of defeating Malvel. The Dark Wizard has won.*

CHAPTER ONE

DECEIVED BY MALVEL

Tom took a short run, pushed off from the ground and soared into the air. Even though he wasn't wearing the golden armour, he had not lost its special powers.

But as Tom landed, pain stabbed through his leg. He looked down and saw that a sharp rock that jutted out from the ground had torn through his trouser leg and cut his calf. He could have sworn that a moment ago there hadn't been any rocks ahead. But then things were never quite as they seemed in Malvel's kingdom.

"What's the matter?" Elenna asked, riding up on Storm, with her wolf Silver loping alongside.

"I cut myself on a rock," Tom explained. "I'd better heal it before we go any further."

Tom removed his shield, which he carried over one shoulder. It held the six tokens that he had won from each of the good Beasts of

Avantia. Tom took out the talon of Epos the flame bird; it felt warm in his hand as he passed it across his bleeding calf. At once the blood stopped flowing and Tom's skin drew together until there was no sign of the wound.

"Impressive," Elenna smiled.

As Tom replaced the talon, he felt a tingling in his shield. Sepron the sea serpent's tooth was vibrating again. The good Beast was being held captive by one of Malvel's evil Beasts, and Tom wondered what shape his enemy would take this time.

"Let's get moving," Tom urged, clenching his fists. "Sepron is still in trouble, and while there is blood in my veins I won't let him die!"

Malvel had imprisoned the good Beasts in Gorgonia, leaving Avantia defenceless without its guardians. Tom knew the Dark Wizard planned to send his own evil Beasts to conquer the peaceful kingdom.

"Let's have another look at the map," Elenna suggested, "and make sure that we're heading in the right direction."

Tom took the map out of Storm's saddlebag, shuddering as he unrolled it. Malvel had sent

the map to Tom and Elenna when they first
arrived in Gorgonia. Made from the skin of a
dead animal, it smelled disgusting, as if it
were rotting.

Elenna looked over Tom's shoulder as he
traced a glowing green line that appeared
on the map. It showed a route through
gentle-looking fields ending at the Black
Ocean, where a tiny picture of Sepron was
now etched.

"We have a long way to go," Elenna said.
"But at least the path ahead looks easier. Fields
all the way to the sea."

"Maybe things aren't all bad in this place,"
Tom said, shaking away thoughts of the next
Beast he would have to fight. "Let's go!" He
stowed the map in the saddlebag again and
strode out confidently along the track. Elenna
urged Storm into motion and Silver bounded
alongside them.

As the day wore on, Tom found that the
track didn't take them across fields but wound
upwards into craggy hills that grew steeper and
rockier with every step. Storm picked his way
carefully among the boulders, letting out

whinnies of protest when sharp stones stabbed
his hoofs. Silver whined softly as he tried to
find a flat spot to set down his paws.

"I don't understand this," Tom said, gazing
around. "Have we come the wrong way?"

"This is the only way we *could* have come,"
Elenna replied. "The track didn't divide
anywhere."

Shaking his head in confusion, Tom pulled
out the map again. "Look," he said. "We
should be on flat ground now. The map shows
green fields."

Elenna looked bemused. "Why does it show
fields if there aren't any?"

"Think about it for a second," Tom said, rage
flooding through him as he realised what had
happened. "Who gave us this map?"

"Malvel." Elenna's voice was tight with anger.

"Right," said Tom. "We must have been
stupid to think we could ever trust it."

Elenna brought Strom to a halt. "We should
stop," she suggested. "The map could be
leading us in circles."

"There's one thing I *do* trust." Tom dug deep
into his pocket and pulled out the compass left

to him by his father, Taladon. He held it in front of him, pointing it up the track.

Elenna leaned over Storm's head to look, and Silver darted around Tom's feet excitedly.

The compass needle was swirling backwards and forwards between *Destiny* and *Danger*.

"Does that mean we'll face both if we go this way?" Elenna asked.

"Yes, it must." Tom stowed the compass away again and straightened up, squaring his shoulders determinedly. "We'll keep going. We have to save Sepron – and ignore Malvel's tricks."

Follow this Quest to the end in NARGA THE SEA MONSTER.

Win an exclusive
Beast Quest T-shirt and goody bag!

In every Beast Quest book the Beast Quest logo is hidden
in one of the pictures. Find the logo in this book and
make a note of which page it appears on.
Send the page number in to us.
Each month we will draw one winner to receive
a Beast Quest T-shirt and goody bag.

Send your entry on a postcard listing
the title of this book and the winning
page number to:

THE BEAST QUEST COMPETITION:
SKOR THE WINGED STALLION
Orchard Books
338 Euston Road, London NW1 3BH
Australian readers should email:
childrens.books@hachette.com.au

New Zealand readers should write to:
Beast Quest Competition
4 Whetu Place, Mairangi Bay, Auckland, NZ
or email: childrensbooks@hachette.co.nz

Only one entry per child.
Final draw: 31 October 2009

You can also enter this competition
via the Beast Quest website: www.beastquest.co.uk

Fight the Beasts,
Fear the Magic

www.beastquest.co.uk

Have you checked out the all-new Beast Quest website?
It's the place to go for games, downloads, activities,
sneak previews and lots of fun!

You can read all about your favourite Beast Quest
monsters, download free screensavers and desktop
wallpapers for your computer, and send
beastly e-cards to your friends.

Sign up to the newsletter at www.beastquest.co.uk
to receive exclusive extra content and the opportunity
to enter special members-only competitions. It's the best
place to go for up-to-date info on all the Beast Quest
books, including the next exciting series,
which features six brand new Beasts.

Series 1

Ferno the Fire Dragon	978 1 84616 483 5
Sepron the Sea Serpent	978 1 84616 482 8
Arcta the Mountain Giant	978 1 84616 484 2
Tagus the Horse-Man	978 1 84616 486 6
Nanook the Snow Monster	978 1 84616 485 9
Epos the Flame Bird	978 1 84616 487 3

Vedra & Krimon: Twin Beasts of Avantia	978 1 84616 951 9

Series 2: The Golden Armour

Zepha the Monster Squid	978 1 84616 988 5
Claw the Giant Monkey	978 1 84616 989 2
Soltra the Stone Charmer	978 1 84616 990 8
Vipero the Snake Man	978 1 84616 991 5
Arachnid the King of Spiders	978 1 84616 992 2
Trillion the Three-Headed Lion	978 1 84616 993 9

Spiros the Ghost Phoenix	978 1 84616 994 6

Series 3: The Dark Realm

Torgor the Minotaur	978 1 84616 997 7
Skor the Winged Stallion	978 1 84616 998 4
Narga the Sea Monster	978 1 40830 000 8
Kaymon the Gorgon Hound	978 1 40830 001 5
Tusk the Mighty Mammoth	978 1 40830 002 2
Sting the Scorpion Man	978 1 40830 003 9

All priced at £4.99

Vedra & Krimon: Twin Beasts of Avantia and *Spiros the Ghost Phoenix* are priced at £5.99

The Beast Quest books are available from all good
bookshops, or can be ordered direct from the publisher:
Orchard Books, PO BOX 29, Douglas IM99 1BQ.
Credit card orders please telephone 01624 836000
or fax 01624 837033 or visit our website: www.orchardbooks.co.uk
or e-mail: bookshop@enterprise.net for details.

To order please quote title, author
and ISBN and your full name and address.
Cheques and postal orders should be made payable to 'Bookpost plc.'
Postage and packing is FREE within the UK
(overseas customers should add £2.00 per book).

Prices and availability are subject to change.